FIND YOUR WAY TO

FIND YOUR WAY TO

By **Lara Bergen**

Based on the motion picture
screenplay by **David Koepp**
and the novel *THE LOST WORLD*
by **Michael Crichton**

GROSSET & DUNLAP • NEW YORK

Warning: SOMETHING HAS SURVIVED!
Don't Go Anywhere Until You Read This....

Are you ready to take the trip of a lifetime (and then some)?

Then begin reading on page 1. Keep reading until you come to a page where you are asked to make a choice. Decide what you want to do, and then turn to that page. Keep reading and making choices until you come to THE END. Now one adventure is over. But there are plenty of others to choose, too. Go back to where you started. A brand-new adventure is waiting to begin!

"Welcome to Jurassic Park San Diego!"

The giant sign looms above you. Too bad the park's not open yet. It would sure make your family vacation to San Diego a whole lot more exciting. Imagine! Real, live dinosaurs to see—and even touch! And your parents thought the zoo and Sea World were cool?

Luckily, your parents are so busy checking out the barnacle exhibit down by the naval shipyards, they didn't even notice when you wandered off. You have hours, for sure, before they even *start* to get a clue.

If only you could get inside this place. There's got to be at least one dinosaur in there for you to see. After all, the posters all around town say, "Opening Soon!"

But hey! Wait one minute. Could it be? A hole in the fence?

Go to page 2.

It certainly is. And there's no one around. This is the chance of a lifetime, and you're going to take it!

You climb through the gap in the chain-link fence and look around. What a mess. There's construction equipment everywhere. And still not a soul. Maybe the barnacle exhibit wasn't such a bad idea, after all.

Then you spy the big concrete building off to your left. It looks kind of like those old Roman…whatchamacallits…amphitheaters? It's not finished, either. But it definitely looks like the main attraction. You might as well check it out while you're here.

Then all of a sudden, you hear a terrifying noise. It's somewhere between a primeval scream and a thunderous roar.

It's your mother calling you!

If you answer, meekly, go to page 7.

If you decide you've come too far to turn back now—and foolhardily ignore her, turn to page 13.

You grab a paper towel and hold it up to your nose. Then you blow—hard.

"Here," you say, handing Sarah the moist rag.

"Uh, thanks," she says a little hesitantly. But it works. The makeshift splint is in place!

Then suddenly, a deafening roar sounds from the jungle (or make that just outside the trailer!), followed immediately by a crashing sound. You whirl and look out the barred windows...straight into the eye of a fully grown T-rex. The baby's mother has come to get it!

"Quick!" Sarah shouts. "Let's let it out to see its mom."

While Nick tries to get the whole thing on videotape, you open the door for Sarah, who shoos the baby out. You quickly slam the door back shut—but outside you can hear the mother rex's cooings and snufflings as she inspects her little baby—and then the *THUD* of their footsteps as they move away.

Phew! That was close! you think.

Now go to page 4.

But the fun's not over yet!

A moment later, something *HUGE* smashes into the side of the trailer. The mother rex has come back to teach you guys a little lesson. No one messes around with Junior!

You look out the trailer window and see the rex getting ready for another charge. You've got to do *something*—and quick!

Your eyes dart around the trailer cabin and quickly light on both the satellite telephone and the ship-to-shore radio. You only have time to try calling for help on one. Which will it be?

If you say telephone, go to page 48.

If you say radio, go to page 54.

You turn the corroded key, and instantly the dinghy's engine comes to life. Bingo! You head straight for the waiting island, full throttle.

It's not long before you find yourself at the shore of a tropical lagoon. A brilliant crescent of white sand stretches out in front of you, bordered by lush jungle fringe. You drive your boat right up onto the beach and happily step ashore. *Now what?* you wonder. Where do you go from here?

You figure you might as well take in the length of the beach. Maybe your mom will be a little easier on you if you bring her back a really cool shell.

As you round a curve in the shoreline, you spy a huge, pearly conch shell. That was easy! But just as you bend down to pick it up, a rustling sound from the jungle draws your attention.

If you turn to investigate, go to page 46.

If you choose to ignore the sound and focus on the prize at hand, go to page 36.

So you think just maybe you're not up to this task? Are you kidding?! Are you really going to chicken out of the chance of a lifetime?! I didn't think so.

Taking a deep breath, you turn and walk slowly toward the cage. It is a *cage,* after all. It's designed to keep things—like dinosaurs—*in.* And things—like you—*out.* What are you so worried about?

You're just a step away. And then it happens. Something grabs you on your shoulder—*hard!*

Go to page 19.

"Coming, Mom," you say, smiling meekly. And as you make your way back through the damaged fence, you can almost feel her eyes burning into you.

"How dare you sneak off by yourself like that!" she snarls. "You had us worried sick!"

"Yeah," says your father.

"We've a good mind to cut this trip short and take you home this very afternoon."

"Yeah," says Dad.

Home? you think excitedly. *Your own Sega? Your own skateboard? Your best friend to play with? Yes!*

"But we're not," says your mom. "We promised Great Aunt Gussie we'd spend the weekend at her house, and we can't disappoint her. She told her whole bridge club you were coming and they've rescheduled their tournament just so they can meet you."

Aunt Gussie! You had completely forgotten about *that* part of this "vacation." Talk about *Jurassic* phenomena. It looks like all you can do now is sit up straight, say "Yes, ma'am," and smile while the old ladies pinch your cheeks, as you miserably wait for...

THE END

"So what do we do?" you ask Kelly.

"Just sit tight," she says. "We'll hide in here and go wherever they take us. When we get there, we'll get out and help. My dad will be so surprised!"

Yeah, you bet!

Then you're surprised yourself to hear the sound of voices approaching. "Let's tow 'er to the barge!" someone shouts.

The barge? You mean you're *sailing* to the island? Won't that take a while? "Why don't they just *fly* us there?" you ask.

"Oh, that would disrupt the environment too much," Kelly explains. "This way is much more sensitive."

And much more nauseating! Oh, well. You're in this thing for the long haul now. Better just sit back and try to enjoy the ride. Maybe they've got some games on these computers....

Challenge Kelly to some electronic hand-to-hand combat, and go to page 9.

The next day, the boat—and you—arrive at your destination. Isla Sorna.

"Yippee!" cheers Kelly.

You stay hidden inside the trailer, however, until it's loaded off the ship and taken to a place a little farther inland. Not until you're positive everyone has headed off into the jungle for their first expedition do you come out of the tiny bathroom.

"Now," says Kelly, "let's get to work. My dad's probably going to be starving when he gets back. I think I'll start a little campfire and make some dinner. Want to help?"

You point out that there's a perfectly good little stove aboard the trailer. But Kelly seems bent on doing the cookout thing.

If you feel like giving Kelly a hand, go to page 10.

If you'd rather get back to the intense game of Double Doom you found on the computer, go to page 43.

You step out onto the edge of a steep, grassy plain over-looking the island's jungle interior on one side and the lagoon on the other. It's a pretty spot, and you can't help singing as you help Kelly build the campfire: "The hills are alive—"

"*Shhh!*" Kelly tells you suddenly.

"Sorry!" you huff. You know you're not the greatest singer, but does she have to be so rude?

Then you realize what she's really talking about. The jungle is moving! A flock of birds shrieks and bursts out of the treetops as a whole section of the forest seems to come to life.

"S-s-s-omething's c-c-oming!" she stutters

Quick! Think fast! Pick a number between 1 and 10.

If you picked an odd number, go to page 53.

If you picked an even number, go to page 18.

Cave B, did you say?

You try to hold your breath and keep your cool at the same time, as you follow Stark past the rotting flesh, and up to the mouth of the cave. From inside the cave, you hear the oddest high-pitched sound.

"What in the—" begins Stark. But before he can finish, he's pelted in the forehead by an unidentified flying bone—"*Ouch!*"—and passes out cold.

You're *this* close to making a retreat, but as usual, your curiosity gets the best of you and pulls you, cautiously, toward the beast responsible for all this mystery...not a T-rex...not a raptor...not even a schizophrenic Triceratops. No, you, my friend, have discovered the world's only living cave man! Talk about theme park attractions—wait until the kids back home get a look at this guy!

You take your hairy friend back to San Diego with you—and become his agent. The talk shows, product endorsement, and book and movie gigs start rolling in, and you soon quit school, move into your own apartment, become rich beyond your wildest dreams, and not until you're one hundred does your long and happy life finally come to...

THE END

"Wow!" says Kelly, running up to get a closer look at the strange creature. It's about the size of a giant carnival teddy bear—with a great big head and great big hungry eyes.

"Yeah, 'Wow,'" repeats Dr. Malcolm. "That's how it always starts. The screaming and running come later."

"What is it?" Kelly asks, ignoring him.

"It's a baby T-rex, Kelly," answers the woman. Obviously, she knows Kelly from somewhere else. "We found it in the jungle. I'm pretty sure its leg is broken—and if we don't set it, it won't stand a chance of surviving in the wild."

As it's carried into the trailer, the baby continues to cry out in pain. And suddenly, Kelly looks a little panicky. "Other animals are going to hear this, aren't they?" she asks, grabbing her father's arm. "I want to get out of here!"

"But you just got here," says Dr. Malcolm.

"No, I mean out of *here!* I want to be somewhere safe. I want to be somewhere *else!*"

"See, I told ya," Dr. Malcolm says with a sigh. "Screaming and running. They're never far behind." Then he grabs Kelly's hand. "Come on," he tells her. "I'll take you to the high hide. You'll be safe there."

If you're with Kelly and want out of there right now, go to page 22.

If you're determined to help make sure this poor little carnivore can lead a long and productive life instead, go to page 32.

You decide you've come too far to turn back now, and foolhardily, you ignore her. So you keep your parents waiting a few minutes. It's not as if they haven't kept *you* waiting before…like all those times when they were supposed to pick you up from soccer practice….

Instead, you keep heading for the amphitheater.

Inside, it's just like a modern gladiator arena—complete with bleacher-style seats all around, and a row of big cages underneath. *This must be where they're going to have the dino shows!* you figure.

Then you hear it. Another roar. At first, you can't believe how far your mother's voice can travel. Then you realize the sound is actually coming from one of the cages under the bleachers. *Gulp!* Something's in there!

Go to page 14.

Of course, you think you've lucked out! There really *are* dinosaurs here, and you're going to be one of the first—if not *the* first—spectator to see them. And you didn't even have to pay admission!

But then you start to get a sudden case of cold feet. Reading about dinosaurs in books—even seeing computer-generated simulations in movies—is a little different from meeting them *in person!*

What do you say? What do you do? Maybe this isn't such a good idea, after all?

**If you think just maybe you're not up to this task,
go to page 6.**

**If you think there's no way on this earth you're
going to miss this opportunity, go to page 17.**

Hey, you've got nothing to prove—and a (hopefully) long, productive life ahead of you. You humbly retreat while you still can—out of the amphitheater, and back toward the gate where you came in.

But now the awful noise is following you. Or is it something else?

Oh, no! It's your Mom! In all the excitement, you completely forgot that she was on the rampage herself. Maybe an angry, hungry dinosaur wasn't such a bad fate, after all.

But it's too late. She's spotted you. And she's giving you that "Get over here this instant, or die!" look. You know you have no choice.

So just smile meekly, and go to page 7.

You guess, logically enough, that the flip of a switch will get the dinghy's motor up and running—and so you flip it. Instantly, you hear the purr of an engine. All right! Then you notice the big red label by that switch you just flipped. "Emergency Submerger," it reads. You have just electronically opened a huge hole in the bottom of the boat...and you are sinking. *What kind of a dinghy is this?* you wonder. But then again, what kind of a dingbat flips a switch before reading the label?

Brrr! That water's cold. And are those big gray fins you see swimming toward you?

I'm afraid that they are—and unless you have inflatable undies and some shark repellent, this is, unfortunately, for you...

THE END

Of course there's no way on earth you're going to miss this opportunity! You head straight for the cage where the noise is coming from. But now it's getting louder. And angrier. And *hungrier!*

By the time you reach the outside of the cage, you can hardly hear yourself think above the noise. But it's so dark inside the cage, all you can see is a big, dark hole. If you're going to see inside, you're going to have to get up *close.*

Of course, it's not too late to turn back, you know....

If you choose to humbly retreat while you still can, go humbly to page 15.

If you choose to boldly ignore your fears and take a look inside, go boldly to page 27.

"Who started a *campfire?*" an angry voice calls out.

"Dad!" cries Kelly happily. "I was just going to make you dinner."

Suddenly, a tall man dressed all in black limps out of the forest. "Kelly!" he exclaims. Instantly, you recognize him from TV—Dr. Ian Malcolm—that crazy scientist who tried to tell people years ago there actually was an island full of man-eating dinosaurs. With a father like that, no wonder Kelly is so nutty. "What are you doing here?" he yells.

"You practically *told* me to come here," Kelly replies. "Remember? You said, 'Don't listen to me.' So I didn't. And here I am. *And* I brought a friend."

"Well you and your friend are going right back where you came from," Dr. Malcolm says. He ducks into the trailer and comes out with a bright green satellite phone.

"Am I at least grounded?" Kelly asks.

"I'll think about it," says Dr. Malcolm.

"Yippee!" Kelly cheers.

You, on the other hand, just sit quietly and wait for her father to call a helicopter to take you back to San Diego. If you're lucky, your parents will only ground you for *ten years!* Who knows, in fact, if you'll even live to see...

THE END

You're spun around—and suddenly you're face-to-face with a mean-looking man in an expensive-looking safari suit. Instantly, you recognize him from the cover of *Time* magazine. It's Peter Ludlow, the man who's responsible for this whole theme park.

"Exactly *what* do you think you're doing here?" he growls.

"I...uh...I..."

But Mr. Ludlow isn't finished. "This place is *totally* off-limits until opening day," he tells you. (As if you didn't know.) "Tell me, what have you seen?"

"N-n-nothing," you stammer. And Peter Ludlow looks relieved. But then, like a fool, you say, "I only heard—"

"*Heard?!*" he cries. "You *heard* something!"

Uh-oh! It looks as if you've said the *totally* wrong thing.

"Er...no! I didn't hear *something*," you blurt. "I heard...nothing. Yeah...that's it...nothing...."

But it's too late. Mr. Ludlow wasn't born yesterday. You, my friend, are in deep dino doodoo.

Go to page 20.

"You're coming with *me*," Peter Ludlow snarls as he grips your shoulder more tightly and leads you off toward the far side of the amphitheater. "I'm afraid we can't have youngsters running around telling people about what they've *heard,* until Jurassic Park is one hundred percent up and running."

"But I won't tell anyone. I promise!" you plead.

Peter Ludlow just shakes his head. "I'd like to believe you. Really I would," he says. "But I have too much at stake. I might as well tell you—what you heard was a very...hungry...dinosaur. A Velociraptor, to be precise, whose keeper, unfortunately, got a little too close. Naturally, if the authorities found out that our attractions were consuming the staff, we'd be out of business before we even opened. And that would cost little old me quite a bundle! But not to worry. We'll see that the Velociraptor is put out of commission. There are many more species, after all, to bring back here from Site B."

"Site B?" you ask.

Go to page 21.

"Yes, Site B!" Peter Ludlow's now on a roll, and there's no stopping his villainous monologue. "Several years ago, John Hammond, my uncle, had a dream—to open the world's greatest theme park—an actual island inhabited by living, breathing dinosaurs. Of course, like Uncle John himself, that dream was entirely impractical, and the whole thing soon got completely out of hand. But that's just because he wasn't working with a controlled environment—like we have here at Jurassic Park San Diego.

"Luckily, Uncle John also set up another island just for breeding dinosaurs—Site B on Isla Sorna. When a hurricane wiped out the whole facility, the animals were all released to mature there on their own—and today what exists is a true Lost World. A complete Jurassic ecosystem—worth millions! I am on my way there now, in fact, to collect our main attractions. And because I can't risk leaving you here to spoil my grand opening—you, my friend, are coming with me!"

Do you dare try making a run for it while you still can?

If dare you do, kick the villain in the shins and run like crazy—while turning to page 55.

If you're not up to taking on a grown man twice your size, be a good little captive, and go to page 39.

You follow Dr. Malcolm and Kelly out of the trailer and across the camp to a complicated structure that Eddie, the equipment guy, has just finished putting together.

"What's this?" Kelly asks as you climb into the metal cage.

"It's a high hide," says Dr. Malcolm. Then a soft, whirring sound begins as the winch lifts you up fifteen feet above the ground. "It's the safest place you can be," he assures you. "See these trees growing all around it? They're poisonous, and animals know it. The plants' strong scent keeps them away. Feel better?"

"Not really," says Kelly. "All I can think about is all those horrible dinosaur stories you told!"

"Oh, those...well—"

"And that big head staring straight at us."

What? You turn to find yourself face-to-face with a full-grown version of that thing still howling in the van. Looks as though one of these freaks of nature was born without a sense of smell. Go figure. It obviously has a sense of *taste,* however—and slowly bends over to give you a warm, slimy lick. Is that a *smile* you see? Well, as Kelly and Dr. Malcolm look on in helpless horror, at least you can be comforted by the knowledge that you taste good as you face...

THE END

"How 'bout a walk through that high grass over there, Mr. Stark?" you ask.

"What? That elephant grass? Are you crazy?" says Stark. "Who knows what you'll meet in there."

Big deal, you think. Like you're worried!

You tromp off into the grass and leave Stark to try to piece together his busted snagger pole.

But you don't get far before you notice a rippling along the surface of the grass. Funny. It doesn't seem that windy. And wonder what those long, lizardy tail-like things are poking up all over?

Not...raptors!

AGHH!

You take off running toward the only gap you can see in the circle of skinny tails. You can hear the raptors snarling and snapping as they chase after you like scaly torpedoes. The tall grass slaps at your face and blinds you, but you know better than to stop. Faster and faster you run—until you feel like your heart and lungs are going to explode...and the ground underneath your feet suddenly disappears!

Go to page 34.

Aboard the ship, Ludlow shows you to your very own stateroom—complete with fruit basket—and tells you not to come out until he says so. He really *isn't* very nice, is he?

You don't have long to think about that, though, because the next thing you know, the floor beneath your feet is shifting and the ship is setting off. It's not long before the whole room seems to be rocking...and rolling...and rocking...and rolling...through the mighty Pacific Ocean. *Uh, oh!* you think. Here comes that corn dog you had for lunch....

After what seems like hours of hurling, you lie down on your bunk and try to get some rest. It's starting to get dark outside your porthole, and you're sure to have a *big* day ahead of you.

Have sweet dreams, and go to page 25.

BRRUMMM! What's that sound? Thunder? You sit up and look out of your porthole. The sky is perfectly blue. And the water's pretty calm, too, all around that island. *Hey!* you realize. *The ship has stopped!* You've arrived at Isla Sorna!

As you finish waking up, you realize that that booming sound you hear is coming from above. On deck, probably. You get up and try the doorknob. Yes! It's unlocked. You grab a bunch of grapes and a banana from the fruit bowl, stuff them in your pockets for later, and open the door slowly. There's no one around. You follow the red exit signs and head up to check it out.

Up on deck, you see the source of all the racket: three enormous military-looking helicopters. The word "InGen" is written on their tails. And it looks like they're getting ready to take off.

Everyone on deck is so busy running around, loading equipment onto the choppers, they'd never notice if you sneaked over to one and slipped into its cargo hold.

But then you notice that dinghy over there next to some crates of Dino-Chow. You could always hop in it and row over to the island all by yourself, take a look around, then row back at your leisure.

What'll it be?

If by air, go to page 30.

If by sea, go to page 50.

"Uh, sure I'll be your scout," you say. After all, it's not exactly an offer you can refuse.

"Excellent," the man responds. "By the way, I don't believe I've formally introduced myself. Roland Tembo—world-famous hunter. And this is my old friend and partner, Ajay Sidhu." He nods toward the man next to him, and then his icy glare returns. "Now, break's over!" he shouts. "Somewhere on this island, there exists the greatest predator that ever lived. And the second greatest predator—*me!*—must take him down. Move on!"

Boy, this guy is pretty heavy, you think. And so is his gear! Because the next thing you know, you realize "scout" is really another word for beast of burden, as you're loaded down with backpacks that feel like they're filled with solid lead.

You follow the two hunters into the dense jungle. Then suddenly, you feel the ground start to shake...*BMBB!*

Roland and Ajay stop in their tracks.

"Did you—"

"Uh-huh."

Quick, go to page 40.

Hey, what can you say. Once again, foolish curiosity triumphs over good old common sense. Boldly, you step up to the bars of the cage and look inside.

Suddenly, the noise you've been hearing stops. Peering into the darkness, you can just barely make out an upright form—about five feet tall, with long limbs and beady eyes staring straight at you! Funny—they're a lot more human-looking than you thought they'd be.

"Hi!"

You jump back. For sure, a *talking* dinosaur was the last thing you thought you'd find!

"Oh, I'm sorry. I didn't mean to scare you," it says. Then a shuffling sound tells you it's moving toward you.

You take another step back and wait with bated breath to see what exactly is coming to meet you.

Go to page 28.

Imagine your surprise to see it's not a talking dinosaur at all—but a young girl.

"What are *you* doing in there?" you ask.

"Oh, I was just playing around with these dinosaur recordings," she explains as she opens the door and steps out into the sunlight. "I'm quite precocious, you see." And suddenly you realize that she wasn't in a cage, but in some kind of high-tech audiovisual control room.

"I'm Kelly Malcolm," she goes on. "And I'm actually on my way to help my dad on an extremely important mission."

"What kind of mission?" you ask.

"Well, I'm not exactly sure," she admits. "In fact, my dad doesn't exactly know that I'm going with him. But I'm so tired of never, ever being punished—you know? I figure if I stow away, maybe he'll crack down on me for once, and even ground me or something. All I know is that they're taking this amazing camper with all this cool equipment—that's what I'm stowing away in—and that they stopped here on the way from New York to get some more supplies. Hey, would you like to come along? It could be fun!"

If you simply can't resist taking Kelly up on her exciting offer, go to page 33.

If you simply can't help thinking that anyone who would actually *want* to be punished must be certifiably insane, go to page 38.

Are you crazy? You're not going anywhere—except into that barge.

Now get into that barge! And go to page 24.

It's now or never, you decide—and make a dash for the choppers. Made it! You scramble in behind a big box marked "DANGER: EXPLOSIVES" and duck out of sight. Minutes later, you're five hundred feet in the air, headed straight for the interior of Isla Sorna.

The choppers land in a small clearing, and there's a frenzy of activity as men and equipment are deployed. No one even notices as you climb out of your chopper and take a look around.

Then you freeze as you hear someone call, "Hey—kid!" Are they talking to you? You slowly turn around and see a stern-looking man staring straight at you. "Don't just stand there," he growls in a funny accent. "Get busy!" He must think you're one of the crew!

"Uh...uh..." you stammer stupidly. "I...I..."

"Don't tell me you don't have anything to do!" he shouts. "*I'll* give you something to do. My driver, Carter, seems to have disappeared—so *you* can drive the snagger."

Drive? You don't even have a learner's permit! And what's a "snagger," anyway? But there's no time for questions, because Mr. Accent is now in your face.

"On the double!" he shouts. "Mr. Ludlow wants this job done A.S.A.P.! By the way, my friends call me Dieter—but you can call me Mr. Stark."

Go to page 31.

Mr. Stark leads you over to a gargantuan jeep and shows you to the driver's seat. *How are you ever going to drive this thing?* you wonder. But you've watched your parents drive plenty of times. Step on the gas. Steer the wheel. What could be easier?

"What are you waiting for?" Stark asks as he picks up a long, thin pole with a noose dangling from one end (Ah—the *snagger!*) and climbs into a little sidecar built onto the jeep. "Let's go!"

You grab the key waiting in the ignition, turn it, and feel the engine come to life. So far, so good! Then you gently press down on the gas pedal. *What power!* you think, as the vehicle takes off under your control.

Then you realize that the jeep is going *backwards*. You had it in reverse! And the next thing you know, your beautiful new jeep is a mass of *olive-drab crumpled* steel, and Mr. Stark is practically foaming at the mouth.

"You idiot! Have you never driven a car before? *Now* what are we going to do?"

Fear not, Mr. Stark. You have several options!

You could take advantage of this beautiful island and take a nature walk through that high grass over there—and go to page 23.

You could see where those *very* deep three-toed tracks you just noticed on the ground lead —and go to page 35.

Or you could stay right where you are and wait for the rest of the hunting party to come back —and go to page 45.

You watch as Kelly and Dr. Malcolm race out of the trailer and over to a metal cage set on tall stilts that Eddie, the equipment guy, has just finished setting up—then you dash over to the metal dining table, where Sarah and the photographer are trying to make a splint for the baby rex.

"Can I help?" you ask.

"I'm almost done," says Sarah as she fits an aluminum foil cuff around the baby's broken limb. "I just need another adhesive. Something pliable...hey, you don't have any more gum, do you, Nick?" she asks the photographer.

"Sorry," he says. "I gave Ian my last piece."

Sarah's eyes dart around the trailer. "What'll we do?" she moans.

Go to page 3.

Naturally, you can't resist taking Kelly up on her kind offer. Important mission? You're there!

You follow Kelly out of the amphitheater and to a huge hangar near the waterfront. Inside sit two long trailers connected by an accordion-like passageway—kind of like on a subway. "This is it!" says Kelly.

She looks around to see if anybody's watching. You seem to be all alone for the moment, so she quickly opens the door in the front of the trailer and waves you inside.

The inside of the trailer's even cooler than the outside. It looks like the bridge on the *Star Ship Enterprise!*

"What is all this stuff?" you ask.

"Oh, computers and lab equipment and that kind of thing. We're going here," she says, pointing to a tiny island on a large electronic map along one of the walls. "Isla Sorna. To study the wildlife."

Study the wildlife? Sounds more like a field trip than an important mission. Maybe you made a mistake....

If you think you have better things to do than go on a nature walk with a stowaway, go to page 42.

If you have a feeling this machine was intended to do more than just observe Dodo birds, go to page 8.

Fate has blessed you with a steep hillside, and now you find yourself in a fifty-mile-per-hour—and rather painful—freefall. When you finally come to a stop, you stagger to your feet and are more than relieved to find that not only are you uninjured, but the raptors did not follow you over the cliff.

When you look around, you see you're standing in a flat, sandy area lined with boulders. It stretches out as far as you can see. But that's not what amazes you so....

Straight in front of you is a row of desks and a big blackboard. Your teacher is standing in front of it, staring at you...hard.

"You're late!" she snaps. "Did you forget about our test today? I certainly hope you studied."

Test? What *test?* Was there supposed to be a *test?*

Or is this just some crazy dream you're having in the safety of your bunk on the cargo ship?

It's hard to tell. All you know is that these desks are pretty hard—and this test is even harder. And as far as nightmares go, this is only...

THE BEGINNING!

"Why don't we just follow these *very* deep three-toed tracks on foot, Mr. Stark," you suggest.

"*Hmm*, interesting," says Stark, picking up his snagger pole. "Let's go."

Together, you make your way through some fairly dense jungle—and then into a small clearing, where a pair of caves is carved into the face of a small mountain and the huge tracks suddenly stop. The ground outside the caves is littered with half-eaten animal remains—arms...legs...heads...you name it...all crawling with disgusting maggots and flies. The stench is almost overwhelming.

"Bingo!" says Stark. Then he pulls up a handful of grass and releases it into the breeze. It floats back between his legs. "This is good," he says, gripping his snagger more tightly. "We're downwind, which means whatever's in there hasn't smelled us yet. We have the element of surprise to our advantage!"

"But there are two caves," you say. "Which one do we look in first?"

If you pick cave A, go to page 56.

If you pick cave B, go to page 11.

So the jungle rustled. Big deal! It's probably just the wind. Right now you're much too focused on getting that cool shell to be distracted.

You happily pick it up to admire it in full sunlight. Oh, yes! Your mom is going to love this. Maybe you should even get a few more? After all, you can never have too much bargaining power.

Then, just as you're stuffing another shell into your pocket (it's getting kind of full by now), you hear it again. It's definitely a rustle. Maybe it's not the wind.

You turn toward the thick jungle curtain. A large bush, maybe twelve feet tall, is swaying. And it's definitely *not* from the wind. Something is coming right at you. And boy, does it smell!

Go to page 37.

You're all set to run for your life, when out of the jungle crashes the source of all that shaking and swaying Two grouchy men. *Ugh!* More grown-ups!

"Who are *you?*" roars the larger one. His steely eyes fix on you with the look of someone used to eyeing prey. It's clear from his camouflage outfit and heavy gear that this guy means business.

You're in no shape to tell this guy who you are. But luckily, he doesn't seem to care. "You haven't seen a T-rex come by here, by any chance, have you?" he asks. "We're trying to tag a bull. But every time we get close, Ajay here's cheap aftershave gives us away." He turns to glare at his partner, a wiry Indian man a few years his junior. "When I gave that stuff to you for Christmas, I never thought you'd really wear it!" he growls.

So *that's* what smells!

"Say," the man goes on, "you look like you have a good head on your shoulders. How'd you like to be a scout?"

If you have a good enough head on your shoulders to know there's no way you can say "No" to this guy, go to page 26.

If you have a good enough head on your shoulders to know there's no way you can hang around that cheap aftershave a second longer, go to page 52.

Obviously, anyone who would actually *want* to be punished must be certifiably insane—and not the best choice in traveling companions. Besides, you know your parents would *more* than ground you if you skipped town on them completely.

You graciously decline Kelly's offer and wish her a *bon voyage*.

Unfortunately, certifiably insane people such as Kelly do not take rejection lightly. The odd glint in her eye tells you that maybe—just maybe—you have made a serious mistake. And as she approaches with her arms outstretched, you wonder: Is this just her crazy way of saying good-bye...or is this, in fact...

THE END

Peter Ludlow leads you out of the amphitheater and over to the docks where a huge cargo ship is waiting.

Okay, hotshot. So maybe *now* is the time for a getaway...?

If you think now *is* the time for a getaway, go to page 29.

If getting away doesn't compare to the chance to see an island inhabited entirely by real dinosaurs, go to page 24.

The hunters pause to listen, and for a moment there's no sound.

"I think we're okay," Ajay says.

And then it starts again. *BMBB!*

No, we're not okay! you think. And you're right—because if you're not mistaken, there, straight ahead of you, is a great, big, enormous, gigantic Tyrannosaurus rex!

You can't help it. You start to scream: "*Agghh!*"

"Shhh!" Roland claps his hand over your mouth. "I don't think he's smelled Ajay yet. We must be downwind. You just sit tight and let me take care of this. Here, rexy, rexy," he coos.

As you stand there quaking in your hightops, Roland raises his huge gun to his shoulder, takes aim, and…

Click.

What? Your jaw drops open, and so does Ajay's, as Roland cracks open the gun and looks inside.

"It's empty!" he shouts.

"You didn't load it?" asks Ajay.

"Of course I did!" says Roland. "It's that good-for-nothing, animal-rights-loving photographer, Nick van Owen! I knew I never should have let him watch my gun while I used the latrine!"

Go to page 41.

You're really starting to panic now. But you try to control yourself. You know such mighty hunters must have more than one weapon on them—or at least some more ammunition stored somewhere. Right?

Wrong.

"Then what's in all these packs?" you ask them.

"Oh, our various hunting awards, plaques, trophies, and the like," says Ajay. "It's all very impressive."

Great! you think. Now you can *impress* the rex to death. And you better start quick, 'cause he's heading straight for you!

"Let's get out of here!" you shout. "Maybe we can outrun him!"

"No way," says Roland, shaking his head. "We've never run from any animal before—and we're not going to start now. Right, Ajay?...Ajay?"

Unfortunately, Ajay cannot answer because that rex was hungry—and stinky aftershave or not, he just made Ajay his first course. Now he's eyeing an entrée of Roland à la King. And it's pretty safe to say that for our two great hunters, this is now...

THE END

But not for you! Quick! Run to page 51.

Too late! You hear voices approaching, and the next thing you know, the trailer is moving. You're being towed somewhere, and at a fairly speedy rate.

Kelly can tell that you're a little nervous. "Don't worry," she tells you. "This is going to be fun! Want a Twinkie?" She opens a cabinet in the galley part of the trailer. To your delight, it's filled with all your favorite snacks!

Wow! It's like junk food heaven. You reach for a Snow Ball and tear off the cellophane wrapper. Then you sit back down on the bolted-down sofa and try to enjoy the ride.

Now go to page 9.

"Uh, you go ahead without me," you tell Kelly. "I'll be out in a little while."

"Suit yourself," she says, and you watch as she steps out of the the trailer and moves off toward the jungle to collect wood for the fire.

You turn away from the window, grab a bottle of juice from the little fridge, and sit yourself down in front of one of the big computer screens. You're whipping the computer's butt, when all of a sudden, you hear a blood-curdling shriek.

Cool! That's a computer sound you've never heard before! Then you notice the liquid in your juice bottle quivering. *BMBB! BMBB!* What in the world could make the ground shake like that?

You run to the door of the trailer to see what Kelly's doing out there. But when you look outside, she's nowhere to be found. "Kelly!" you call. But the only reply is a deep, thunderous "*BURRRPP!*"

You turn toward the sound—and are frozen by what you see. An enormous Tyrannosaurus rex—you'd know one anywhere!—with just a little bit of what looks like blue jeans dangling from its ferocious jaws.

Don't just stand there! Go to page 44.

You slam the trailer door and run to crouch in a corner. But not before the T-rex sees you. Through the window, you watch it lower its head, denim still dangling from its teeth, and peer inside. When its huge eye spots you, it makes a roar so loud and low, it rattles everything in the trailer that isn't bolted down—including you!

You pinch your arm and tell yourself to wake up from what has to be a terrible dream. Unfortunately, you're as awake as you'll ever be—and you won't be for very long, because the T-rex has already started tearing apart the trailer. And if this prehistoric can opener has its way—as they usually do—this is most unfortunately...

THE END

Why not just stay right where you are and wait for the rest of the hunting party to come back? How long could it take? And in the meantime, maybe you can even break through your pal Dieter's tough-guy exterior and find out a little more about what this trip is about.

"Want a grape?" you ask him, pulling the bunch you smuggled off the ship out of your pocket.

"*Mmm!*" He smiles. "Don't mind if I do."

Little do you know that the place you've picked for your siesta is on one of the island's most popular *game trails,* belonging to one of the island's most popular *carnivores*—the Tyrannosaurus rex. Did you know that their teeth are seven inches long? Well, you will...because it's getting close to dino feeding time....

Hey! What's that growling noise and rustling in the bushes? Sorry to say, it sounds like for you, dear reader, the beginning of...

THE END

Choosing to investigate, you turn toward where the thick jungle foliage gives way to the white sand. A large bush, maybe twelve feet tall, is swaying—and not from the breeze! Curious, you move closer. Then suddenly it stops and a small animal steps out from behind. It's dark green with brown stripes along its back like some kind of exotic lizard, only it walks upright and bobs its head just like a chicken! You've definitely never seen anything like it before—and yet there's something strangely familiar about the cute little critter.

"Well, hello there!" you say. But the animal just stares at you.

"Are you hungry?" you ask. Then you reach into your pocket and pull out the bunch of grapes you carried with you from the ship. Not too smashed, you notice happily. "How 'bout a grape?"

You pluck off one and offer it to the little guy. Interested, it stretches out its head and takes a sniff...then a taste. "*Blagh!*" The lizard spits it out almost automatically, and the grape goes rolling off behind you.

"Fine!" you huff. "Get your own food, for all I care." And you turn back to look for that shell.

Go to page 47.

But soon a soft chirping sound and then a louder rustling make you turn back toward the jungle again.

"What the...?" There, where the lone lizard had once stood before, now stand thirty or more exactly like him!

Heads bobbing, they start drawing closer...and closer...and that's when you realize why the creature seemed so familiar to you. You *have* seen it before. In your *Deluxe Encyclopedia of Dinosaurs!* These things aren't lizards—or bald chickens. They're Compsognathi (or compys, for short)—one of the smallest, and *hungriest,* meat-eating dinosaurs ever found.

Now they're hopping up and down and chirping excitedly before you. You feel like an ice-cream truck surrounded by kids on a hot summer day. Or maybe make that the ice cream itself!

You take a step back...then another...and another. If you can just make it back to your boat, you'll be home free. But the compys keep right up with you.

No more playing it cool, you turn and *run.* And you almost make it! But I'm afraid you underestimated the determination of hungry compys. And as you feel the very first of their tiny sharp claws land on your back, you know fairly certainly that this is...

THE END

You grab the satellite phone out of Sarah's lucky backpack and dial the only number you know to call in serious emergencies: 911.

"Hello?" says the operator. "How can I help you?"

"Well, you see, we're in this fancy trailer on an island near Costa Rica," you explain quickly, "and we're being attacked by a very angry Tyrannosaurus rex. What do we do? What do we do?"

"Stay calm," the operator urges you, "and tell me exactly what the rex is doing."

"Well, she's roaring, and drooling, and she's ramming into our trailer with all her might," you say.

"I see. And is she showing any signs of tiring?"

BOOM! "Definitely not!" you scream.

"Okay. Then it looks like you'll have to calm her down yourself. Don't worry. I'll talk you through it. Just do exactly what I say. Can you do that?"

"I think so...."

Now take a deep breath, and go to page 49.

"I need you to sing the dinosaur a lullabye," the operator says calmly. "Do you know 'Rock-a-bye Baby'?"

"'*Rock-a-bye Baby*'!?" you exclaim.

"Yes, it's their favorite."

Is this some kind of joke? you wonder. But you really don't have much choice—because Mrs. T. is bearing down on you once again. You can practically feel her hot breath wafting over you....

"Rock-a-bye baby, in the treetops...."

Suddenly, the T-rex stops. She cocks her head and softly closes her mighty jaws, and the next thing you know, she's snoring like Great Aunt Gussie in-between bridge hands.

"...cradle and all," you finish. "She's asleep!" you tell the operator. "We did it!"

"Good work," she commends you. "I'm just glad I could help."

Meanwhile, Nick and Sarah can't believe their eyes. You alone (with the help of the 911 operator) have tamed the savage beast—and with just a few bars of "Rock-a-bye Baby" in three-quarter time.

What happens next? Well, you go back to Jurassic Park San Diego, become a world-famous dinosaur trainer, and send your parents off on endless vacations—alone! Congratulations on doing so well for yourself in...

THE END

So what if you've proven that you're hopelessly sea-sick. You've also had as much of mean grown-ups as you can take for one adventure. (Who knows what that crazy Ludlow would do if he found you?) And you'd much rather take your chances out on your own. You haven't got any more lunch to lose, anyway.

While the ship's crew finishes getting the choppers ready, you head the other way, toward the dinghy. It's a nice one—with a motor and everything.

You hop on in, and with the flip of a switch, a winch starts lowering you down to the water. Piece of cake! But how do you start this thing?

If you guess by the turn of a key,
go to page 5.

If you guess by the flip of another switch,
go to page 16.

Way to run! But don't you know no one can outrun a hungry T-rex? And this one still has room for dessert!

For him, it's the end of another fine meal.

And for you, well, it's just plain...

THE END

"I'm sorry," you say. "My mother told me never to go hunting large game with strangers."

"No matter." The guy shrugs. "Probably best to keep the hunting party lean, anyway. Shall we head on, Ajay?"

"After you, Roland," replies his friend.

"No, after you."

As you watch the pair troop back into the dense jungle, a part of you is sorry to be missing this big chance. Imagine hunting down a real Tyrannosaurus rex...*Tyrannosaurus rex!* On second thought, you're probably better off on your own. You quickly set off in the opposite direction.

Then, just a few yards away, you notice some extremely large impressions made in the sand. They look a lot like giant bird tracks. Actually, if you didn't know better, you'd think they were..."Hey, guys!" you start to yell.

Then you feel it. *BMBB! BMBB!!* The very ground beneath your feet is trembling. It's almost like an earthquake...an earthquake that's getting closer!

You turn to run, but before you can take a step, a gigantic, snarling head bursts out from the bushes. You try to yell, "T-rex over here!" But you never get the chance—because, believe it or not, for you this is...

THE END

Suddenly, a dark green Mercedes Benz all-activity-type vehicle bursts through the trees and a tall man dressed in black steps out. Instantly, you recognize him from TV—Dr. Ian Malcolm—that crazy scientist who tried to tell people years ago there was actually an island full of man-eating dinosaurs.

"Dad!" cries Kelly happily.

"What are you doing here?" he yells.

"Making you dinner," she replies. "After all, you practically *told* me to come here. Remember? You said, 'Don't listen to me.' So I didn't. And here I am. *And* I brought a friend."

But before Dr. Malcolm can respond, another AAV drives up and three more people get out: a young man with about a hundred cameras strapped around his neck; another man loaded down with electronic equipment straight out of a science fiction movie; and a pretty young woman with a pretty disgusting-looking backpack—carrying some kind of screaming, wounded animal in her arms.

"No lectures, please, Ian," she says.

Go to page 12.

You lunge for the elaborate radio console built into the wall of the trailer and hit a series of switches. The console blinks to life—Hooray!

You pick up the transmitter and turn up the volume dial...

La bamba!

Who was listening to salsa music and forgot to set the radio back to the right frequency? You're gonna kill 'em!

But you really don't have time to worry about that stuff right now, because—*BOOM!*—the rex has just hit you with charge number two! And boy was it a doozy! The entire trailer turns over. There's an earsplitting *CRACK!* of electricity. Everything goes black. And the trailer jolts into motion, sliding forward.

"Oh, no!" cries Sarah. "They're pushing us over the cliff!"

Cliff! What cliff?

That cliff right behind you, stupid. The cliff you're going to tumble over in just a minute.

Maybe you should have tried the phone. Maybe then you could have called someone to rescue you. But it's too late now. All you can do now is sit back and enjoy the ride while you wait for...

THE END

"*Owwww!*" howls Ludlow as he lets go of your shoulder and grabs his shin in agonizing pain.

Your toe doesn't feel too hot either, but it sure doesn't stop you from hauling your butt out of that amphitheater—and fast! Too bad you can't remember exactly where you came in. Was it over there to the left? Or over there to the right? Or maybe right there in front of you? It's worth a shot, you figure....

Until you get close enough to realize that where you're headed is straight for the raptor's cage—the *hungry* raptor's cage. And since we're on the subject—the hungry raptor's *open* cage!

How did that happen? you wonder. But unfortunately, you'll never know—because for you, dear reader, this is definitely...

THE END

Cave A, did you say?

You try to hold your breath and keep your cool at the same time, as you follow Stark past the rotting flesh and up to the mouth of the cave. From inside the cave, you hear the oddest high-pitched squeaking sound.

"Why don't you go in first," suggests Stark, nudging you ahead of him with his snagger pole. *Now* he gets polite!

You continue on into the cave—as quietly as you can—until you're stopped by a dried mud wall. You climb up to the top—and what you see on the other side almost makes your heart stop. It's some kind of nest—about ten feet wide and lined with bones of every shape and size. And what's in it? Either the biggest, ugliest alien in the universe—or a baby Tyrannosaurus rex!

You're so amazed by what you see, you don't even hear Stark scream out a warning from below. And the next thing you know, something pushes you into the nest.

When you look up, you see the mother T-rex staring down at you. When you look back down, you see the baby toddling eagerly over to you—kind of like a little kid running for a cookie. In fact, if you didn't know better, you'd think the baby thought you *were* a cookie...a big, juicy, meaty cookie! And if I didn't know better, I'd have to say your young, bakery-fresh life has come to...

THE END

Look for these other exciting books:

THE LOST WORLD: JURASSIC PARK™
The Junior Novelization

THE LOST WORLD: JURASSIC PARK™
The Movie Storybook

The Dinosaurs of
THE LOST WORLD: JURASSIC PARK™
An All Aboard Reading™ Book

THE LOST WORLD: JURASSIC PARK™
Role-Playing Book